For Elizabeth Dalton
A.D.

The King's Toothache
Text copyright © 1987 by Colin West
Illustrations copyright © 1987 by Anne Dalton
First published in England by Walker Books Ltd, London
For information address Harper & Row Junior Books,
10 East 53rd Street, New York, N.Y. 10022.
Printed in Hong Kong by Sheck Wah Tong Printing Press Ltd.
First Harper Trophy edition, 1990

Library of Congress Cataloging-in-Publication Data
West, Colin.
    The king's toothache.

    Summary: Unable to find a dentist for the king's
toothache, Nurse Mary tries a baker, a town crier, and a
sailor before the poor man gets relief.
    [1. Kings, queens, rulers, etc.—Fiction.
2. Toothache—Fiction.   3. Stories in rhyme]   I. Dalton,
Anne, ill.   II. Title.
PZ7.W51744Ki 1988   [E]   87-3713
ISBN 0-397-32251-8
ISBN 0-397-32252-6 (lib. bdg.)

    "A Harper Trophy Book."
ISBN: 0-06-443168-1 (pbk.) 87-8416

THE KING'S TOOTHACHE

WRITTEN BY
Colin West

ILLUSTRATED BY
Anne Dalton

A Harper Trophy Book

Harper & Row, Publishers

At Kennelwick Castle,
Gadzooks and forsooth,
The King has a terrible
Ache in his tooth.

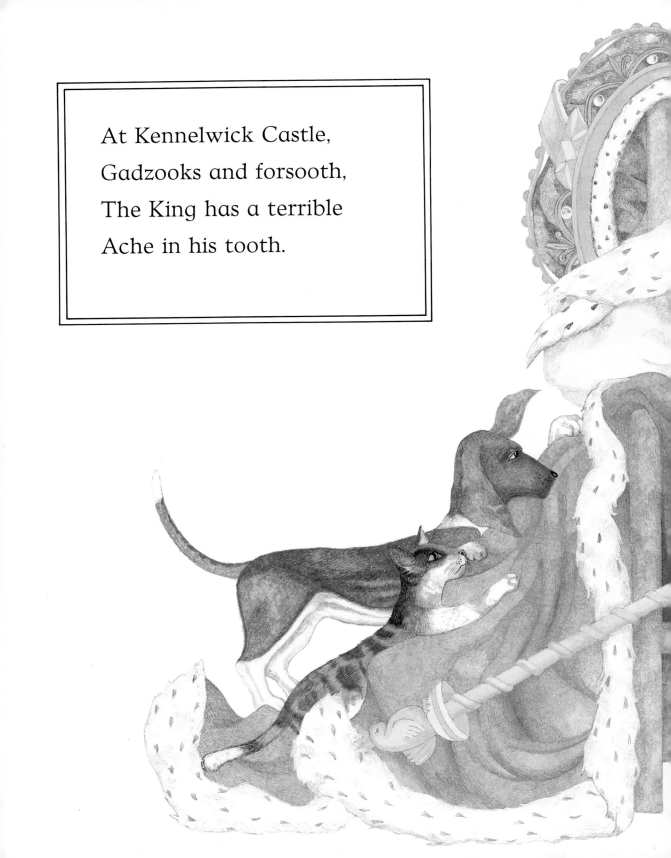

"Go fetch me a dentist,"
 He moans to his nurse,
"And hurry up, Mary,
 Before it gets worse."

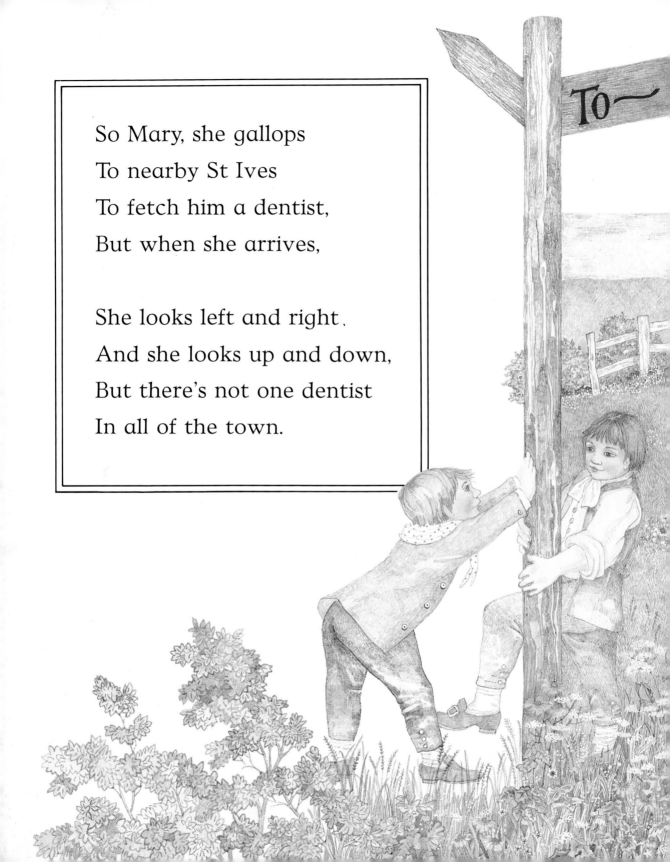

So Mary, she gallops
To nearby St Ives
To fetch him a dentist,
But when she arrives,

She looks left and right.
And she looks up and down,
But there's not one dentist
In all of the town.

So Mary, she stands
And she scratches her head
And decides to return
With the baker instead.

At Kennelwick Castle
The King's tooth still aches.
The baker comes in
With a trayful of cakes.

The King eats them up,
But they don't do the trick:
His tummy now aches
And he's feeling quite sick.

"Go fetch me a doctor,"
He moans to his nurse,
"And hurry up, Mary,
Before it gets worse."

So Mary, she gallops
To nearby St Ives
To fetch him a doctor,
But when she arrives,

She looks left and right
And she looks up and down,
But there's not one doctor
In all of the town.

So Mary, she stands
And she scratches her head
And decides to ask back
The town crier instead.

At Kennelwick Castle,
To make the King well,
The town crier lets out
A deafening yell.

The King isn't cured, though,
And takes to his bed,
For now he's complaining
Of aches in his head.

"Go fetch me a surgeon,"
  He moans to his nurse,
"And hurry up, Mary,
  Before it gets worse."

So Mary, she gallops
To nearby St Ives
To fetch him a surgeon,
But when she arrives,

She looks left and right
And she looks up and down,
But there's not one surgeon
In all of the town.

So Mary, she stands
And she scratches her head
And decides to go back
With a sailor instead.

At Kennelwick Castle,
The sailor he looks
Deep down the King's mouth,
And with twine and with hooks

He finds the bad tooth
Which he waggles about,
Then he tugs on the string
And he pulls it clean out.

He then pours a potion
And though looking glum
The King drinks it down
And it cures his bad tum.

Then singing a shanty
And dancing a jig,
The King throws his headache
Away with his wig.

He hasn't a worry,
He hasn't a care,
He's fit as a fiddle
And dancing on air.

"Three cheers for the sailor
For all that he's done,
A dentist and doctor
And surgeon in one!"